CHAPTER

1

THE BEGINNING OF ME!

A doodle of me

Ok. Starting from the VERY beginning, I was born on

3 **27** **2017**

◉ at home.

✓ in a hospital.

◯ in a birthing pool.

◯ in the car on the way

☐ home.

☑ to the hospital.

☐ to the birthing pool.

◯ (other)_____.

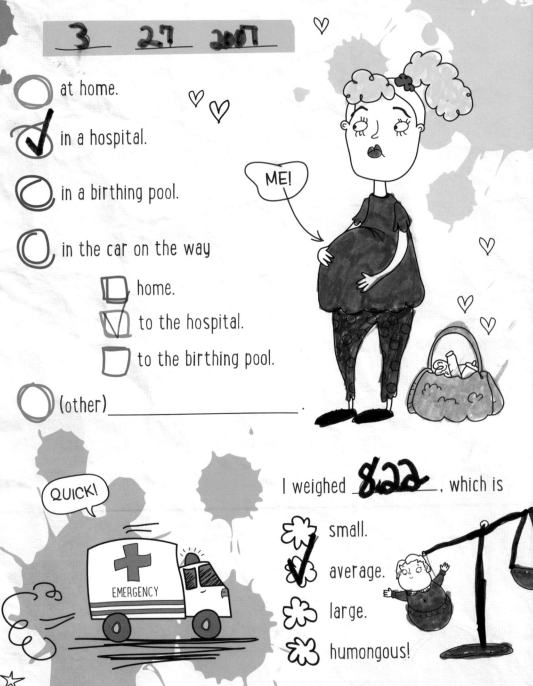

ME!

QUICK!

EMERGENCY

I weighed **8.22**, which is

❀ small.

✓ average.

❀ large.

❀ humongous!

According to Mom, when I was born, I . . .

☐ was like a angel.

☑ made far too much noise.
(Nothing changes, apparently.)

☐ looked like Grandad.

☐ had **big** hair like Tina Turner*
in the 1980s.**

Grandad! :-o

This is **Tina Turner.**

She had
BIG hair!

Here I am when I was a baby! I think I look . . .

● CUTE.

○ LIKE AN ALIEN.

○ LIKE A CUTE ALIEN! :-)

○ LIKE TROUBLE.

Mom looking angry.

(I'm prob being noisy!)

* A famous rock star when your mom was a kid.
** A really long time ago.

MY NAME

After **much discussion and soul searching** / very little thought,

I was named*...

Rate it out of 10.

First name:
EMILY

$\frac{}{10}$

Middle name:
Paige

$\frac{}{10}$

**Middle name (Yes, I have two /
If I had another, it would be):**
margret

$\frac{}{10}$

Last name:
BUCK

$\frac{}{10}$

My name written in the petals of a flower. :·)

If I could go back and **secretly** give my parents a
NAME-CHOOSING SERUM that would mysteriously
make them choose the names I would want when I was older,
this is what would happen:

☆ I would still have the
names I've got.

✗ I would have the same name
but with this modification:

_____

☆ I would have a TOTALLY
different name:

_____

The magical name serum! :-O

A teeny
weeny
ladybug!

Here are ten names, from my **favorite** right down to one that
I wouldn't wish even on my worst enemy!

1) Elizabth

2) Jayh

3) Paige

4) A Ann

5) Mary

6) Mary

7) wasiton

8) pom

9) stamper

10) patrick

Definitely the BEST
name ever!

The worst
name
EVER!

Sooooo
embarrassing!

If I had been a boy, maybe
I would have looked like this!

Ha, ha! :-0

* If I had been a boy, I would have been called:

Hunter

Out of 10, this name gets: 10

It's quite possible that one day I will be a HUGE celebrity, so I'll need to practice my autograph! :-)

They say your handwriting says a lot about you.

My signature will say that . . .

I am fabulous. ☐

I am mysterious. ☐

I am notorious. ☐

My autograph in loopy writing.

My autograph incorporating hearts and stars!

My autograph in spiky writing.

Dead famous

OMG!

Can you guess who?

Obviously, **if / when** I become HUGELY famous, my phone will be filled with the numbers of my celeb friends!

These will include . . .

talor swift ♥

Andy Grammer ♥

megedhraioar ♥

Arionaananda ♥

Junst'nbever ♥

mom ♥

Dan ♥

♡rothers ♥

talor swift — Hi B*f

mc — HI B*F

This is a photo of my

FAVORITE

celebrity of all time

with a doodle of ME

next to them

so that we look like

BEST FRIENDS!

My **mom** was _____ years old when I was born, which means she was born in 19____!

I did a little online research and can confirm that my mom was born in the same year as the following **famous people**! :-)

1. _great_ How cool is that?

2. _great_ How cool is that?

3. _great_ How cool is that?

This is what my mom used to wear when she wanted to look SUPER-COOL as a teenager.

Gorgeous!

If my mom wore **any / all of that** to my school TODAY (like, the 21st century), I would be

And this is how she did her hair!

so proud. :-)

unbothered.

slightly embarrassed.

MORTIFIED! :-0

or something else

I am **an only child / one of** kids!

I get along with my siblings

famously.

averagely.

terribly.

I already said I don't have any!

BACK TO **ME** . . .

MY FAMOUS FIRSTS

(as I remember them)

Technically these may not be my firsts. But they are the firsts I **remember**.
Calling this my "**FAMOUS SECONDS OR THIRDS, MAYBE**" would be
factually correct but not as **snappy** title-wise.

My first **FRIEND** Nina

My first **ENEMY** Megan

Love going on
vacation! :-)

My first **VACATION** Westvagn

The first **REALLY BAD** thing I did Lie

My first **SHOES**
(looked like this, probably)

♡ ubby Sitech

My first
AWARD
was for Gymnastics

Ooh la la!
Now they are
FABULOUS!

My first **SLEEPOVER** Grandmas

My first BOYFRIEND
(Ok, we weren't **literally** boyfriend and girlfriend, **and / but** we **did / didn't** consider getting <u>married</u>.)

Cupid! :-)

A picture of us madly in love!

cute

His name: _____

My first TIME ON STAGE

scard

Also, I **don't** actually remember my first **HAIRCUT**, but when I was little, my hair looked mainly like this:

It's a look I'd call

cute. ✓

random.*

a crime against the small and adorable.
(meaning me, obviously!)

* Random is a great word – it can obviously mean a lot of things. In this context it means it looked as though my mom cut my hair while watching the television and not my head.

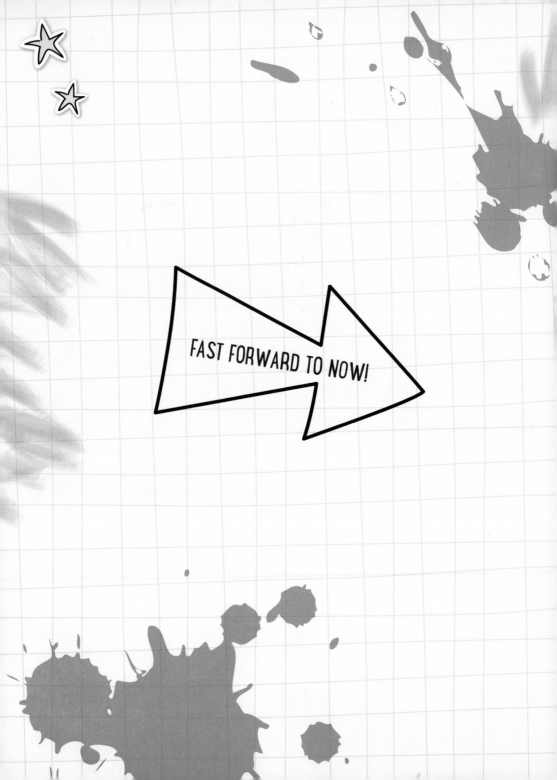

FAST FORWARD TO NOW!

CHAPTER 2

MORE ABOUT ME!

A photo of me!

MY HOME

My address is 1738 State route 534 oenna ohio.

I've lived here for 1 years. I'd describe the area I live in as good.

If there was a "100 Most Desirable Places To Live In The Whole Country" competition, I think my town would probably rank number 10, which is **great / ok / tragic**.

The three **BEST** things about where I live are:

1. windows.
2. fire place.
3. air condishaning

↑ Totally AMAZING!

The three **WORST** things (brutal but true) are:

1. My.Brothers
2. sharing a room
3. room next to brothers.

↑ Oh dear, oh dear.

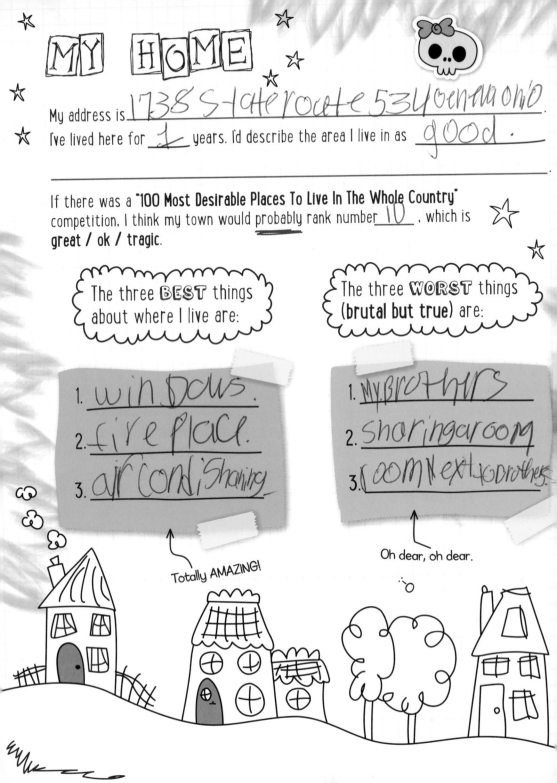

If I could give my town a **MULTI-MILLION-DOLLAR** makeover, thus transforming it, beyond question, into the most **FABULOUS** place to live in the country, the first thing I would do would be *pay someone to Drive me a Limo* closely followed by *pay some money to Drive me* and not forgetting *or I could just walk.*

However, even if **my town** did achieve a **miraculous** makeover, if money was absolutely no object (and I could take all the people I like with me), I would live in

the countryside.

- for the weather ☐
- for the countryside ☑
- for the glamor ☐
- for the peace and quiet ☐
- for the shopping ☐
- for the buildings ☐
- for the excitement ☐
- for the things to do ☐
- for the sports ☐
- for the food ☐

I currently live in a __farm__.
However, during my life, I have also lived in . . .

a house

a boat

a trailer

an apartment

a penthouse

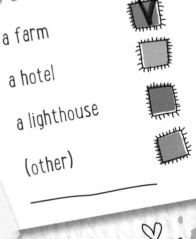

a farm ✓

a hotel

a lighthouse

(other)

_____

My home.

Here's a drawing of my home. I've marked the rooms you can see from the front.

The **best** room is _frontroom_
because _youhaveanic_
veiwoftheroad.

and the **worst** is _Basment_
because _youcan'tsee_
aveinoftheica

MY ROOM

My bedroom is approximately _____ long and _____ wide,
which makes it **huge / big / average / small / a bit like a HUTCH!**

My room is **shared with** _No one_ **/ it's all mine. :-)**

If I were to move to a new house
in a **REAL** hurry, these are the
five things I'd grab from my
room before we left.

Doodles of
the **FIVE** things.

1 BOOK

2 candy per

3 Nail Pali's

iPaD.

4 Note book

5

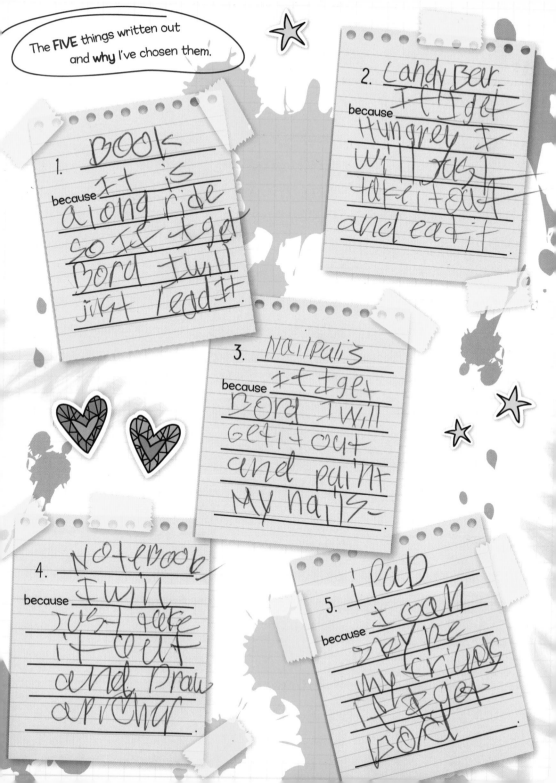

The **FIVE** things written out and **why** I've chosen them.

1. BOOK
because It is a long ride so if I get bord I will jist read it.

2. Candy Bar
because If I get Hungrey I will just take it out and eat it.

3. Nailpalis
because if I get bord I will get it out and paint My nails.

4. Notebook
because I will just take it out and Draw a picter.

5. iPad
because I can type my friends if I get bord.

I keep my room super-neat and clean **all the time (duh)** / **some of the time** / **never, unless under extreme pressure (obviously)**.

These people **are** <u>**allowed**</u> into my room any time they want.

Daddy

Mommy

makenzee

One of these
pictures might
be my best friend!

:-) :-p

However, these people are NOT allowed in. EVER. Well, maybe if they came with a **big gift / scandalous secret / my favorite snack / a new pair of shoes** of my choice.

Lilly.

Abby.

Bri'ah.

TA DAH!

EVEN MORE ABOUT ME

- I am **not** / **usually** / **very** organized.

- I like / **really cannot bear** my books arranged in **color** / **height** / **alphabetical** / **any** order.

Likewise, if you looked in my **cupboards** (which you may do only with my absolute **EXPRESS** permission, by the way), you would be

delighted by the symmetry and order.

(HORRIFIED,)

sick with envy – I am **so** on-trend.

(other) _____ .

My **three** FAVORITE things
in my closet are:

1) MY PanDa t-shirt

2) My Shoes

3) MY Dresses

Quick doodle of them. →

But there will be more about
my **UNIQUE STYLE** later.

Obviously, sleep is very important and I do a lot of it in my bedroom. My bed is **super-comfortable / too hard / too soft / a bit like the bed in the story about a princess and a pea (i.e. lumpy, NOT really tall, with about 50 mattresses).**

Here's a sketch of my **favorite** quilt / bedspread.

And this is a pattern that would look really **cool** on a duvet cover.

If I were to look under my bed, here are the three things I would find (I **think**):

↓ ↓ ↓ ↓ ↓ ↓ ↓ ↓ ↓

WHAT I THINK I'LL FIND	WHAT I ACTUALLY FOUND
1 molly	1 Gams
2 candy	2 trash
3 books	3 cloths

AND THERE'S MORE . . .

CHAPTER 3

MY FAMILY

Love
Love
Love

A lovely doodle of us.

MY FAMILY TREE

Here's **EVERYONE** in my **family** (or at least everyone I can **remember**) on a family tree. Those marked with * aren't actually related to <u>ME</u>, but they feel like family, so for the purpose of this book they are.

This isn't one of those **complicated** FAMILY TREES where everyone joins up, it's a family tree where people's names are written on leaves and if they are **married** or in **love**, their two leaves sit together. <u>How cute is that?</u>

FAMILY STATS

The oldest person.

The **oldest** person in my family is
__Grampa Buek__.
He / she is ___80___ years old, which
is my age multiplied by ___7___.
or in dog years* ___?___.

The youngest person.

The **youngest** person in my family is
___6___ years old. The **difference**
in age between the oldest and youngest
people in my family is ___6___ years.

All my family live in the same **world /
hemisphere / continent / country /
county / town / street / house**.

We get along . . .

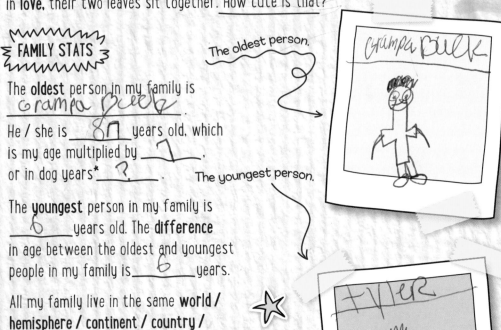

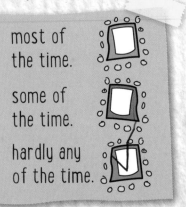

most of
the time.

some of
the time.

hardly any
of the time.

* One dog year = six human years.

If I were to run my own **FAMILY AWARDS CEREMONY** (a bit like the **Teen Awards** or **OSCARs** but on a smaller budget and probably not on TV), here's <u>who</u> would **win** what. In no particular order:

Coolest Relative
Brian

Tallest Relative
Daddy

Geekiest Relative
Tyler

Relative with the Best Sense of Humor
Emily

Relative with No Sense of Humor
Tyler

Relative with the Coolest House
Annaleise

Best-Dressed Relative
Grandad

Worst-Dressed Relative
Tyler

Relative with the Best Hair
Mommy

If I were to be **TOTALLY BRUTAL** and measure my family on an

EMBARRASSMENT-O-METER

So awful!
Oh no! :-{

here's how they'd **shape** up!

Emily
Brian
mommy
Pompy
Ellen
Gramps B
Graeme B
Aunt Ariss
mummy
Grandpa
Grandma
Grandad

Names here →

← Names here

100% COOL!

Ice cold :-)

DEVASTATINGLY
EMBARRASSING!

Bright red embarrassment!

Overall I'd say the **best** thing about my family is *they let me have my own room*
and the most **challenging**[*] thing is *to have my mom nag.*

While I **would not** change my family for the **world**, it's an interesting, if slightly random, pastime to think about who your family would be if every MEMBER was a **CELEBRITY**. Here's who I'd pick as my . . .

famous mom

Yes

famous dad

yes

famous brother

NO

famous sister

yay

famous gran

yay

famous grandpa

NO

famous aunt

yes

famous uncle

yes

famous cousin

yes

[*] *That's a nice way of saying worst, btw.*

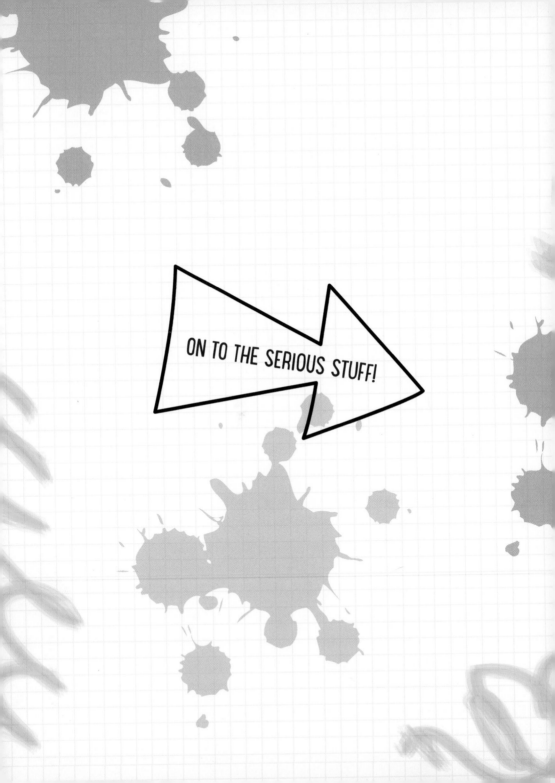

ON TO THE SERIOUS STUFF!

CHAPTER 4

SCHOOL

A doodle of ME in my school uniform.

SCHOOL

If I am NOT at home or with my family and it's a weekday, there is **a very good chance** that I will be at **school**.

Although if the name were to **accurately** describe what it's like, it would be called

My school is called

cork Blamepett

The ladybug is back!

ExHellen

Overall, I'd grade my school . . .

I am in grade _____ and in total have been in this school for _____ years. I think the school has about _____ 200 students. I'd say I know about _____ 50 % of the people in my school and of them I ACTUALLY like **all / about 3/4 / 1/2 / 1/4 / very few / none** of them.

Amazing

A

B

C

D

F

Terrible

Here's a **picture** of my school.

You can

get around easily.

get lost in it. ✓

FRIENDS! :-)

Doesn't it look

inspirational. :-)

interesting.

like a school.

like a prison! ✓

SCHOOL RULES

Schools have rules. I **suppose** that's **important**, otherwise there would be total **anarchy.*** However, I am not in TOTAL agreement with **ALL** the rules at my school.

Here are **three** that I think are totally fair:

and here are **three** that are NOT:

RULES
RULES
RULES

The principal isn't looking too happy! :-[

Yummy cakes!

Here is one that is **fair** but also annoying:

If I were the school **principal** for a day and could make and **enforce as many** rules as I wanted, this is what I **would** do:

A) have no rules. ANARCHY!*

B) make the following school law:

School law by ME!

I hour of Resses for All the grades for ever

The punishment for **not** abiding by my very **fair** rules would be as follows:

1) **worst** possible punishment

geAthGA DeRGon

2) **light** punishment for nothing that bad or maybe doing something by mistake

stey ther Reses.

I stick to the school rules **all the time /
most of the time / occasionally / never.**

The **most trouble** I have <u>ever</u> got into at
school rated on a **TROUBLE-SCALE**
of 1 to 10 as a __! Here's what happened.

This was:

absolutely not
really my fault.

about **50%** my fault.

totally my fault!

The **MOST TROUBLE** I've been
in, ever, was when I . . .

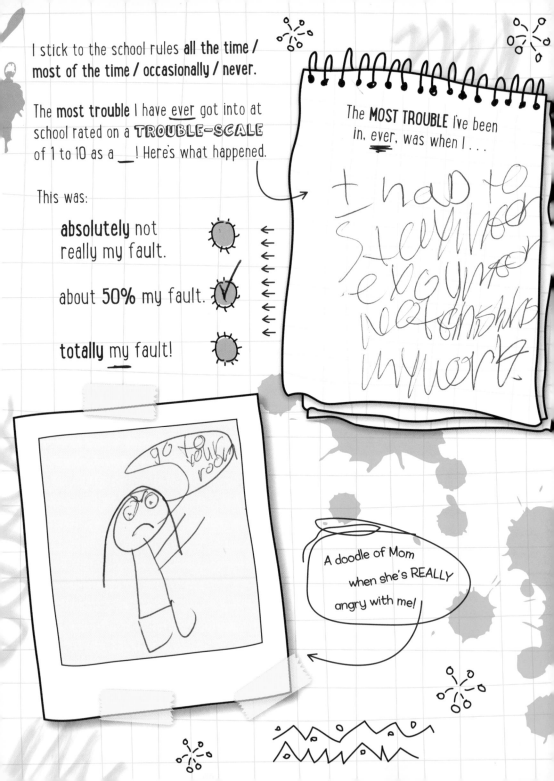

A doodle of Mom
when she's REALLY
angry with me!

Interestingly, while many words have **opposites**, "trouble" **does not**. However, that's **not** to say I don't **frequently** stay out of trouble.

Sometimes / often / to be honest, rarely I win awards, have praise lavished on me and am generally revered.* These times make me **PROUD**.

Here, I share my PROUDEST **school** moment.

She's VERY proud.

Me looking very proud of myself.

*... slight exaggeration, maybe.

A Quick Note About . . . EMBARRASSMENT

What's **worse,**

getting in trouble? ○

suffering a majorly embarrassing incident? ✓

The **main problem** with **EMBARRASSMENT** is you can never **actually** prepare yourself for it. It just happens. I am the sort of person who finds herself taking the bus to **blushville** . . .

on a **regular** basis. During classes, at home, in restaurants – anywhere really. ☐

thankfully **not** very often. ☐

never, I am so together. ☑

WELCOME
to red-faced
BLUSHVILLE
CITY OF EMBARRASSMENT

She's NOT **embarrassed** even though there's BROCCOLI in her hair! :-O

I find that one **positive** way to cope with EMBARRASSING MOMENTS is to tell myself that actually, it could have been SO, SO much **worse**. For example, here are **three** occasions where I broke out in a BLUSH, accompanied by **three** ways in which things could have been so much more **shameful**.

Oh the shame!

Embarrassed face!

1) I went to the bathroom which would have been so much worse if . . .

2) the toilet papper bihind get stuck on my shoe. but it wasn't as bad as it would have been if . . .

3) I was at church but at least . . . I wasent

Obviously, the main point of being in school is to **learn stuff.** I'd say that after ___5___ years in school, my brain is about this full.

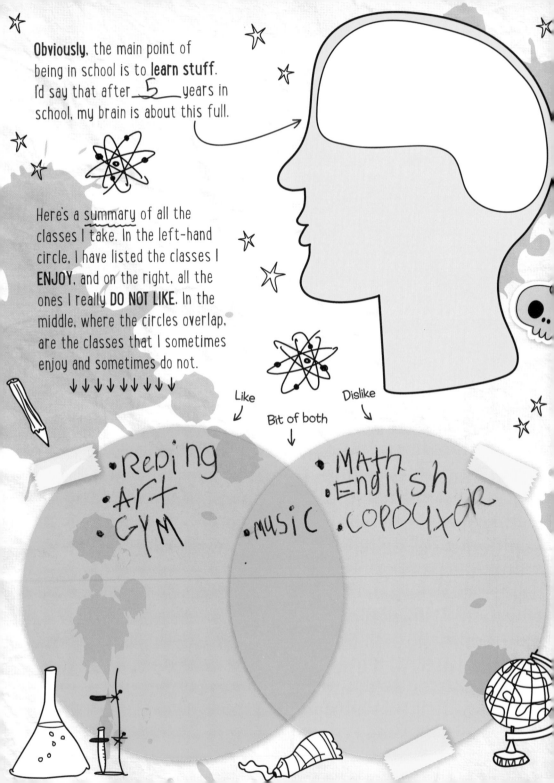

Here's a summary of all the classes I take. In the left-hand circle, I have listed the classes I **ENJOY**, and on the right, all the ones I really **DO NOT LIKE**. In the middle, where the circles overlap, are the classes that I sometimes enjoy and sometimes do not.
↓↓↓↓↓↓↓↓↓

Like
↙

Bit of both
↓

Dislike
↘

• ReDiNg
• ArT
• GYM

• MUSiC

• MATh
• EngLish
• COPDUYXOR

Here are my **FAVORITE** and **WORST** classes at school.

⭐ My favorite class is ┆ 🙂

⭐ for the following reasons:
- Reading
- art
- Gym

⭐ My worst class is ┆ 🙁

⭐ for these reasons:
- Maths
- English
- copouter

SUBJECT	GRADE
Math	C+
English	A+
Music	S
Art	A+
Gym	DX
Reading	DX

Here's a list of my **BEST** and **WORST** grades ever, by subject.

(Just as an aside, I can honestly say that **I have / have never** faked illness to get out of my **worst** class.)

This student is genuinely feeling sick.

ART

On a scale from **1 to 10**, I would rate my artistic skills
(1 being <u>awful</u> and 10 being Pablo Picasso*): $\frac{}{10}$

Which is **good / bad news** as I am about to create **amazing cartoons / terrible drawings** of my two **favorite / least favorite** teachers. :-)

PABLO

Teacher 1

MRS ranDl2

Teacher 2

MrS13

* A very talented Spanish painter and sculptor.

SPORTS

Whilst learning (and socialising) is obviously the MAIN **purpose** of education, there is **a whole lot / a minor amount** of other stuff going on in my school.

For example, **SPORTS**. I participate in the following sports

- **as <u>often</u> as possible.**
- **<u>never</u>, if at all possible.**

People say that with sport it's not the **WINNING** that really matters, it's the "TAKING PART." This is, in my opinion,

incredibly **true** and **wise**.

true **sometimes**, but not always.

100% nonsense – it's all about the prize!

often / never

often / never

often / never

often / never

A doodle of me in my sports uniform! :-)

My **greatest** sporting achievement

The date:

The sport:
GYMNASTICS

The occasion:

I was bursting with pride when ... I won The first Place

My **greatest** sporting disaster

The date:

The sport:

The occasion:

I died of shame when ...

Here are my **TROPHIES**, lined up on my shelves. I cannot <u>honestly</u> say I have actually won **any / all of** the awards inscribed on the front, but I'd **really like to,** which is the next best thing, really.

LET ME ENTERTAIN YOU!

In school / out of school, I am **regularly / never** involved in

plays.

shows.

choir.

Glee Club.

ANY performance type activity is, for me

a chance to shine.

a chance to show off.

a chance to be **really** embarrassed.

During my **glittering** entertainment career I have performed in

My **favorite / worst** role ever was _____.

It was
- indisputably breathtaking.
- really good considering I'm NOT a professional.
- award-winning!
- Mom said great, but I'm not 100% sure she was being totally honest.
- quite good really.
- utterly SHOCKING!

If I were to become a famous **actor / singer / dancer / all-round entertainer** (it could happen), these are the shows I would like to perform in:

<u>CLUBS!</u> I am a member of these clubs:

☼ _____

☼ _____

☼ _____

☼ _____

GLEE CLUB!

The following **clubs** do not exist in **any form** at my school. However, if they did, I would attend them on a <u>REGULAR</u> basis:

☼ _____

☼ _____

☼ _____

☼ _____

LET'S SHIFT THE FOCUS TO . . .

CHAPTER 5

BEST FRIENDS 4 EVER!

MY FRIENDS

A group photo of my _friends_ and **me**.

Here's a diagram (**yes**, you have seen one like this **already**) filled with MY FRIENDS.
On the left are my **school** friends and on the right are my **out-of-school** friends.
In the **middle** are the people who are my friends **both** in and out of school.

School friends

Both!

Out-of-school friends

mahenzee
mabbie
lillian

Mahenzee
lillian

Austen
mabbie .m
mandy
BFF
mandy
BFF

Doodles of my friends!

Mabbie

Mahenzee

Lily

Here they are again, this time entered onto my **CHARACTER CHECKLIST**. This is an
epically useful tool if I need to **quickly** find someone who, for example, likes **sports**
but is also FASHION-SAVVY, or KIND but also **sarcastic**. I have, of course, filled the
table out with nothing but **LOVE**. If any of my friends see this and **don't** like it,
what are you doing **looking** in my journal anyway?

Tick the yellow boxes!

CHARACTER CHECKLIST

↓↓↓↓↓↓↓↓↓↓

Names	Characteristics (e.g. funny)				
Mandy					
Makenee					
Lily					
Mehazer					

FUN GAMES!

FRIENDS 4 EVER!

Ok, so this might sound **a bit weird,** but if I could make a MAXI-PAL MASH-UP,* these are the characteristics I'd take from my friends and bundle together into one brain.

Seeing as that's a slightly **strange** thing to do, I am going to make it slightly **weirder** by inventing a name for my MEGA-FRIEND by mixing up bits of their names, comme ça!**

Mega-friend name! :-)

* Ultimate friend created from my friends' best
** French for "like this"!

Obviously, my friends and I never intentionally do anything that our parents (or other "responsible adults") would disapprove of, although in truth, there are probably other things they would **rather** we did.

This patented <u>PARENTAL APPROVAL-O-METER</u> (look familiar?) shows <u>six</u> things we like to do and how **approving** our parents are of them.

The
PARENTAL
APPROVAL-O-METER

— Definitely approve

Certainly not! —

If we are at school, the day is pretty much mapped out for us and, with the exception of **surprise** fire drills or **real** emergencies, things **usually / often / sometimes / hardly ever** go to plan.

If we're not at school and we can do mostly what we want when we want, a typical day pans out like this.

Morning

Afternoon

Evening

ENOUGH ABOUT THEM . . .

CHAPTER 6

ME
ME
ME

ME
ME
ME

MORE ABOUT ME!

My favorite picture of me! :-)

MY STYLE

I promised, earlier, to talk about **MY PERSONAL STYLE**, which is something that **just happens naturally / I work on really hard / I don't really think about.**

As a **percentage** I am made up of:

- goth **0** %
- skater **0** %
- punk **0** %
- hippy **0** %
- preppy **0** %
- vintage **0** %
- (other) **100** %
  beutiful

Here's a **typical** look for me.

And here's **MY SECRET SIDE** (what I'd wear if I could get away with **anything**).

STYLE AUDIT

This **handy** grid lists all my FAVORITE clothes. The check in the box indicates which tops (shirts, tees, hoodies, etc.) go **best** with which bottoms (jeans, skirts, leggings, etc.).

↓ Tops ↓			← Bottoms →			
Dresses			Legans			
			Jeans			

Here's how my hair looked when I **started school**. :-o

And here's how my hair looks **now**! :-)

CELEBRITY STYLE

Here are **three** CELEBRITIES who I admire for their FABULOUS styles.

Why I **admire** his/her style:

I WANT their clothes!

NAME: _____

LOVE
LOVE
LOVE

Too cool!

NAME: _____

NAME: _____

Why I **admire** his/her style:

Why I **admire** his/her st

BUT, I really **don't like** what these three celebrities choose to WEAR.

Why I'm **NOT** keen:

NO
NO
NO

Why I'm **NOT** keen:

NAME: _____

What were they thinking?

Why I'm **NOT** keen:

NAME: _____

NAME: _____

I ♥ SHOES

This is a CRIME against FASHION!

FUTURE ME

I cannot see into the future, which means I **cannot know** what bad stuff might occur, but similarly, I <u>cannot</u> know what good stuff might occur, so I might as well assume everything is going to be **FABULOUS!** :-)

This is my <u>**POSITIVITY PIE**</u> – it has **six slices,** and each one contains something **FABULOUS** I can see in my future.

A doodle of what **Future Me** might look like.

What I might look like when I'm REALLY o

There is a **WHOLE TON** of stuff / not much that I want to get done in my lifetime but I know **realistically** it won't all happen at once (which is probably a good thing because things might get **complicated** if it did).

So here's a **checklist** of things I expect to have done by the time I am **20**, **30** and **100**. And finally a list of **five** things I <u>never</u> want to do, **EVER**.

By the time I'm **20**,
I will have . . .

* hochlegs
* jumprope
* phone
* cat
* horse

By the time I'm **30**,
I will have . . .

* boy friend
* married
* be a vet
*
*

By the time I'm **100**,
I will have . . .

* Nothing
*
*
*
*

Five things I will
<u>NEVER</u> do!

* flying a
* Air Plale
*
*
*

ABSOLUTELY THE END*

Absolutely Not!!!

* Absolutely not, I have plenty more to write and draw about myself!

School

I am In 4th Grade but

I got this book in 3rd grad
I still have 12 pages I
have to right in the
I am going to make my
own book
about this.
Here is a
dodle of
. Me in school

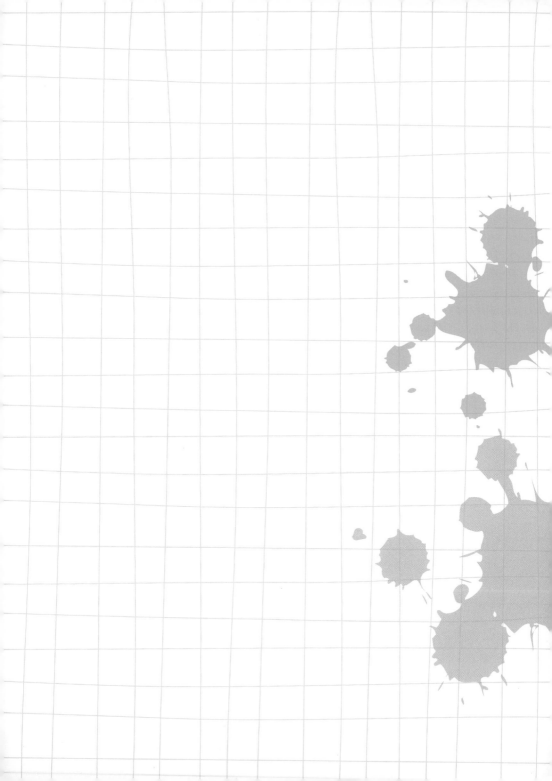